One Night,
One Hanukkah Night

One Night, One Hanukkah Night

by Aidel Backman

The Jewish Publication Society
Philadelphia - New York
5751 - 1990

Text and illustrations copyright © 1990 by Aidel Backman
Design by Edith T. Weinberg
All rights reserved
First edition.
Manufactured in Korea
10 9 8 7 6 5 4 3 2 1

Library of Congress Cataloging-in-Publication Data

Backman, Aidel.
    One night, one Hanukkah night / by Aidel Backman. — 1st ed.
        p.   cm.
    Summary: Each night for eight nights a candle is added to the
great silver menorah. Illustrations depict the celebration in
homes past and present.
    ISBN 0-8276-0368-1 :
    1. Hanukkah — Juvenile literature. [1. Hanukkah. 2. Counting.]
I. Title.
BM695.H3B32   1990
296.4′35 — dc20
[E]   90-4965
                                                                        CIP
                                                                        AC

To the memory of my grandparents whom I never knew:
Aaron and Chana Margolin, Meir and Aidel Schneur

—A.B.

One night

One Hanukkah night.

One night, one light
One shining Hanukkah light
In the great silver menorah

MENORAH—The eight-branched Hanukkah
  candlestick

The SHAMASH is the candle used to light the
  eight other candles in the menorah.

That Zaidy lit
So long ago.

ZAIDY—Yiddish name for grandfather

Second night, two lights
Two shining Hanukkah lights
Giving Hanukkah gelt

HANUKKAH GELT—gifts of money given on
Hanukkah

As Zaidy gave
　So long ago.

Third night, three lights
Three shining Hanukkah lights
Sizzling latkes frying,

LATKES—potato pancakes

As Bubby made
So long ago.

BUBBY—Yiddish name for grandmother

Fourth night, four lights
Four shining Hanukkah lights
Bright dreidels spinning.

DREIDEL—a four-sided top, with a Hebrew let-
ter: Nun, Gimel, Hey, or Shin printed on each
side. The letters stand for "Nes Gadel Haya
Sham"—a Great Miracle Happened There. It
is used to play the game of dreidel.

"Nes Gadol Haya Sham"
A great miracle happened there
For Israel
    Long ago.

Fifth night, five lights
Five shining Hanukkah lights
Remember the
brothers Maccabee

MACCABEES—A small group of Jews, led by
the five sons of the high priest Matisyahu.
They rebelled against the large armies of the
Syrian-Greek King Antiochus and won the
battle.

Who fought the Greeks
So long ago?

Sixth night, six lights
Six shining Hanukkah lights
Singing songs of Hanukkah

As Zaidy sang
So long ago.

Seventh night, seven lights
Seven shining Hanukkah lights
Plays of Hannah's seven sons

Who showed their faith
  So long ago.

HANNAH'S SEVEN SONS—Seven courageous
  brothers who gave their lives rather than bow
  to Greek idols.

Eighth night, eight lights
Eight dancing Hanukkah lights

Hanukkah lights will
always shine
As they did
So long ago.